KU-190-204

# DORRIE

## and the Wizard's Spell

For Dawn and David

# EGMONT
*We bring stories to life*

First published in Great Britain 1974.
This edition first published in Great Britain 2015 by Egmont UK Limited
The Yellow Building, 1 Nicholas Road, London W11 4AN
www.egmont.co.uk

Text and illustrations copyright © Patricia Coombs 1968
Patricia Coombs has asserted her moral rights.

ISBN 978 1 4052 7766 2

A CIP catalogue record for this title is available from the British Library.

Stay safe online. Egmont is not responsible for content hosted by third parties.

MIX
Paper from
responsible sources
FSC® C018306

# DORRIE

## and the Wizard's Spell

by Patricia Coombs

EGMONT

This is Dorrie. She is a witch. A little witch. Her hat is always crooked and her socks never match. The Big Witch is her mother, and Gink is her very own black cat.

One Monday Cook was away and Dorrie was trying to think of something to do, when the Big Witch said:

'I need someone to help me at the Library Bazaar and Tea today. Do you think you and Gink could help?'

'Oh yes,' said Dorrie. 'I would like that.'

Dorrie ran and got her cloak and put it on, and Gink went with her.

The Big Witch tied a sack of things for the Sale
to the broomstick. Dorrie and Gink climbed on the
broomstick behind the Big Witch and they flew into
the air.

Over the house and trees they went, over the marsh
and the pond towards town.

They landed in front of the library right beside
a big sign that read:
BAZAAR AND TEA TODAY

A wizard named Wink was just landing, too.
They said 'HOWDOYOUDO' and went inside.

Dorrie helped the Big Witch put everything out on a long table. There were plates and vases and plants, and bats and balloons and boxes of toads. There were mittens and scarves and skates, and hats and ladles and lace.

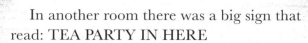

In another room there was a big sign that read: TEA PARTY IN HERE

All the books that began with W were in there. Most of them were Wicked or Witches or Wizards or Worse.

'I like selling things,' said Dorrie.

'And the library will soon have enough money to buy a new glue cauldron,' said the Big Witch, 'and another broomstick holder for the hall.'

Suddenly Wink the Wizard jumped up
beside Dorrie. 'PSSST!' he whispered to her,
'I have something special for you to sell. It is the
strongest Magic I ever thought up.'

Wink the Wizard reached up his sleeve and pulled out a little jar. He put it down beside Dorrie, and before she could ask what sort of magic it was, Wink the Wizard disappeared in the crowd.

Dinger and Squig came. Dorrie showed Dinger an alarm clock.

'I love alarm clocks!' shouted Dinger. 'I will buy it. Now I have seventy-three alarm clocks.'

Dinger was so happy he danced around to the ringing of the alarm clock.

Squig chased Dinger around the room, waving his umbrella at him until Dinger turned the clock off.

Miss Dorp bought a whole box of scarves and gloves and beads and bracelets and bangles.

Squig came back and got a pair of yellow earmuffs to wear in case Dinger started ringing his alarm clock again.

Then he bought three umbrellas.

Mr Obs came by to get new violin strings and a pair of red mittens.

Crowds of witches Dorrie had never seen before came and went, muttering and mumbling and fighting over all the things on the table.

Wizards hurried around with bags and boxes of things they had bought.

Dorrie was very, very busy. The Big Witch was very, very busy.

Soon nearly everything was gone.

The Big Witch sat down and sighed. 'My goodness, I am tired. And I think I am getting a headache. Dorrie, bring me a cup of tea and I will take my headache powder.'

'All right, Mother,' said Dorrie. She skipped
past the chattering witches and wizards into the
Tea Party Room. Gink went with her.

Mr Obs was pouring tea and wearing his new
red mittens.

'Your mittens look very nice, Mr Obs,' said
Dorrie. 'May I please have a nice cup of
tea for Mother?'

Mr Obs poured a cup of tea. Dorrie carried it very carefully back across the room to the Big Witch.

'Thank you,' said the Big Witch. 'Now, if I can just find my headache powder. The jar was right here a minute ago.'

Dorrie and the Big Witch looked all around.

'Oh my,' said Dorrie, 'maybe I sold it.'

'Hmmmm,' said the Big Witch, 'no, here it is.'

The Big Witch put the powder into her tea and slowly drank it.

Dorrie sold two jars of thistle jam, a blue plate and a speckled bat. She helped a nice elderly witch who could not see very well find a pair of glasses. They were sunglasses, but the elderly witch loved them.

Dorrie turned round to show the Big Witch
how many things she had sold. Nearly everything
was gone.

So was the Big Witch.

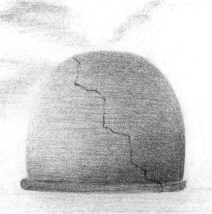

'Mother?' said Dorrie. She looked all around.
She looked under the table.

The Big Witch wasn't there.

'I wonder what happened to Mother, Gink,'
said Dorrie.

Gink blinked and meowed.

Some funny-looking witches came over to Dorrie.
'Pssst!' said one, 'we heard that Wizard Wink left
a spell for sale here. We'll buy it.'

'Oh!' said Dorrie, 'I forgot all about that. It's around here somewhere.' She found the little jar behind a broken teapot and gave it to the witches. They began to fight and screech over it. One of them snatched it and the top flew off. The powder scattered all over them.

One witch stuck out her tongue and tasted the powder.

'Bah! A trick!' she cried. 'It is nothing but headache powder!'

The witches rushed off angrily.

Dorrie picked up the little jar and looked at it.

'Headache powder? But Mother . . . oh no! Oh, Gink, Mother took the wrong powder with her tea!'

Dorrie ran across the room. She ran into the Tea Party Room and Gink went with her. She looked everywhere for Wink the Wizard.

She looked and looked and looked. Finally she saw him sitting on a shelf.

'Wizard Wink,' said Dorrie, 'my mother has disappeared. She drank the spell in the bottle you left, instead of her headache powder.'

Wink the Wizard laughed. He laughed and
laughed and laughed so hard he tumbled off the shelf.

Dorrie was cross.

'Please hurry and tell me what was in that spell.
I have to find my mother.'

Wink the Wizard stopped laughing just long
enough to say:

'It turns witches into whatever they are looking at
when they drink it. Isn't that clever? The Big Witch
will now be a string of beads, or an alarm clock, or
a speckled bat for the next thousand years!'

Wink the Wizard vanished in a puff of smoke.

'Oh, Gink,' said Dorrie, 'we sold Mother to somebody at the Bazaar. We have to find her. But first, I have to remember what Mother was looking at when we gave her the cup of tea. Oh my.'

Dorrie went to Mr Obs.

'Mr Obs!' said Dorrie, 'something awful has happened to Mother. Somebody bought her by mistake.'

Mr Obs dropped his violin. Miss Dorp and Squig and Dinger rushed over to see what was wrong. Dorrie told them how the Big Witch drank the Wizard's spell.

'Hmmm,' said Dinger, 'do you think my new alarm clock is the Big Witch?'

They all looked at the alarm clock very hard.

'I don't think so,' said Dorrie. 'You had already bought the clock when Mother disappeared.'

'Ah,' said Mr Obs, 'perhaps she is a violin string, or my new red mittens!'

'Or my beads,' said Miss Dorp, swinging a string of beads in the air. The string broke and the beads rolled all over the floor.

'Oh, I hope that isn't Mother!' wailed Dorrie.

'Now, now,' said Mr Obs, 'don't worry. We will be very quiet and THINK. What was the Big Witch looking at when Dorrie gave her the cup of tea?'

They all stood still and thought very hard.

'Well,' said Dorrie, 'I think Mother must have been looking at the cup of tea.'

'Hmmmm,' said Squig, 'if that is so, then the Big Witch drank herself, and we will never find her.'

Dinger grabbed one of Squig's umbrellas and pulled it down over Squig's head.

'KEEP STILL! It isn't the TEA, it is the CUP we must find.'

'Of course!' they all said at once.

'It was a white cup with a ring of pink bats round it,' said Dorrie.

They rushed off to find the cup. They looked at the teacups the witches and wizards were holding.

They looked and looked and looked.

Suddenly they saw it. The nice elderly witch in sunglasses had it in her hand.

When the elderly witch saw them running towards her, she gave a shriek and leaped into the air.

The cup sailed out of her hands.

Dorrie made a big jump into the air. She got the cup just before it could smash on the floor.

'Yow!' said Dorrie. 'I'm glad I caught it.'

Dorrie held the cup very carefully in her hands and sat down.

'Mr Obs got the elderly witch another cup of tea. They all said they were sorry they scared her.

The elderly witch in sunglasses sat down beside Dorrie.

'What is so special about that cup, my dear?' asked the elderly witch.

'It's not just a cup,' said Dorrie. 'It's my mother. Wink the Wizard played a cruel trick.'

The elderly witch in sunglasses looked at Dorrie and Mr Obs and Squig and Dinger and Miss Dorp.

'I know a secret,' she whispered. 'I know a secret about Wink the Wizard that nobody else knows. I know because my cousin has a friend who has an uncle who has a niece who used to be Wink's cook. Tell me, my dear, can you make fudge?'

Dorrie shook her head. 'I'm not allowed to use the stove. And Cook is away.'

The elderly witch got up. 'I will help you. Wink cannot resist fudge.'

'Oh,' said Dorrie. 'I hope it will work.'

They all hurried outside to get their broomsticks.

Dorrie and Gink went with the elderly witch, and everyone flew away to Dorrie's house.

Dorrie put on an apron. She got out pots and pans, and sugar and milk and butter and chocolate.

Dorrie and the elderly witch
mixed up a big, big, big pot of fudge.

Squig opened the door so the smell of the fudge would float skyward.

The kitchen grew dark as the fudge slowly cooked.

They poured it into a big pan to let it
cool and then they sat very still and waited.
   'Shhhhh,' said the elderly witch,
'I hear him!'

There was a swish of air outside the door. And suddenly a dark shape grabbed for the pan of fudge. Squig slammed the door and locked it.

Everybody else jumped on top of Wink.
'Fudge! Fudge! Fudge!' mumbled Wink the Wizard.

'I want my mother back,' said Dorrie. 'As soon as you turn this teacup into the Big Witch, you can have the fudge. You can have the whole pan of fudge all for yourself.'

Wink the Wizard licked his lips. 'All of it? I'll do it. Anything, anything at all. You want a witch instead of a teacup. So it shall be.'

Wink took some magic dust out of his sleeve and dropped it into the cup. He mumbled and spun three times.

There was a POUF!

Wink the Wizard and the pan of fudge disappeared.

There stood the Big Witch with a big smile, and her arms round Dorrie.

All that was left of the spell was a small
ring of pink bats round the Big Witch's hat.

'I'm so glad you're home,' said Dorrie.

'So am I,' said the Big Witch. 'Thank you for saving me from the Wizard's spell.'

The Big Witch made a big jug of hot cocoa. They all put on their ice skates and went skating on the pond in the moonlight.

Afterwards, they built a fire and sat round and sang songs until it was time for bed.